KIDS CAN'T STOP READING THE *CHOOSE YOUR OWN ADVENTURE* STORIES!

"I like Choose Your Own Adventure books because they're full of surprises. I can't wait to read more."

—Cary Romanos, age 12

"Makes you think thoroughly before making decisions."

—Hassan Stevenson, age 11

"I read five different stories in one night and that's a record for me. The different endings are fun."

—Timmy Sullivan, age 9

"It's great fun! I like the idea of making my own decisions."

—Anthony Ziccardi, age 11

And teachers like this series, too:

"We have read and reread, worn thin, loved, loaned, bought for others, and donated to school libraries our Choose Your Own Adventure books."

CHOOSE YOUR OWN ADVENTURE®— AND MAKE READING MORE FUN!

Bantam Books in the Choose Your Own Adventure® Series
Ask your bookseller for the books you have missed.

Choose Your Own Adventure Books for younger readers

THE
LOST TRIBE

BY LOUISE MUNRO FOLEY

ILLUSTRATED BY PAUL GRANGER

An Edward Packard Book

BANTAM BOOKS
TORONTO · NEW YORK · LONDON · SYDNEY

RL 4, IL age 10 and up

THE LOST TRIBE

A Bantam Book / August 1983

CHOOSE YOUR OWN ADVENTURE® is a registered trademark of
Bantam Books, Inc. Registered in U.S. Patent and Trademark
Office and elsewhere.

Original conception of Edward Packard

ISBN 0-553-23366-1

Published simultaneously in the United States and Canada

Bantam Books are published by Bantam Books, Inc. Its trademark, consisting of the words "Bantam Books" and the por-
trayal of a rooster, is Registered in U.S. Patent and Trademark
Office and in other countries. Marca Registrada. Bantam
Books, Inc., 666 Fifth Avenue, New York, New York 10103.

PRINTED IN THE UNITED STATES OF AMERICA

O   0 9 8 7 6 5 4 3 2 1

For my friend Charlotte Hutchison
—who passes all the tests

WARNING! ! !

Do not read this book straight through from beginning to end. These pages contain many different adventures you may have in New Zealand as you search for the Lost Tribe. From time to time as you read along, you will be asked to make decisions and choices. Your choices may lead to success or disaster.

The adventures you take will be the result of your choice. *You* are responsible because *you* choose! After you make your choice, follow the instructions to see what happens to you next.

Think carefully before you make a choice! One mistake could be your last . . . or it *might* lead you to the Lost Tribe.

Glossary

adze Axlike tool.
Ariki Chief of the Tribe.
e noho ra Goodbye.
hangi Earth steam oven.
Hohepa Joseph.
kahu Harrier hawks.
kaka Parrot.
marae The village square.
mata-kite Clairvoyance or second sight.
mere Short, flat stone weapon for hand-to-hand fighting.
moa Giant extinct flightless bird.
moko Tattoo on face or body.
Ngatimamoe Eighteenth-century Maori tribe forced by a more powerful tribe to flee to the west coast of the South Island of New Zealand. Now known as the Lost Tribe of Fiordland.
ocher Yellow or reddish clay used as a pigment.
pa Fortified Maori village.
pakeha White person.
rakau whaka-papa Carved stick that tells the tribal genealogy.
taiaha Hardwood two-handed weapon with a long, tapering, flattened blade—broad at one end, with a tongue-shaped spearhead at the other.
tao Shorter spear.
tapu Sacred; forbidden.
tiki Carved image of the first human being.
Tohunga The tribal priest.
totara Forest tree.
whetu Star.
Wiremu William.

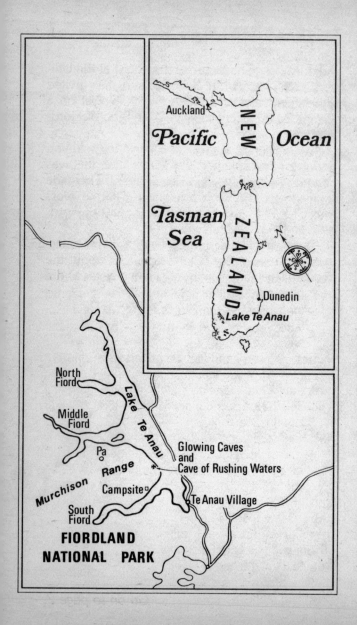

Your uncle Charlie, an archeologist at the University of Dunedin in New Zealand, has invited you to join him and another archeologist on a search for artifacts from the Lost Tribe of Fiordland.

It sounds great to you. Your uncle has told you about the Ngatimamoe, the Maori tribe that was chased by a rival tribe to Lake Te Anau. There the Ngatimamoe lost their last battle. The survivors fled across the lake into the wild forests of Fiordland and were never seen again.

That was two hundred years ago. Even today, your uncle says, the older Maoris talk about the Tribe and tell legends about glowing caves and a cave of rushing waters.

Go on to page 2.

Before you leave, you get a book about the Maoris from the library. You read many interesting things about their way of life and even learn a few of their words, like *pakeha* (white man) and *kaka* (parrot).

By the time you board your plane for the long flight to New Zealand, you have made a decision. You know that parts of Fiordland have never been explored. You will search for artifacts with your uncle. But you believe that the Lost Tribe still exists—and you are going to find it!

Turn to page 4.

Uncle Charlie meets you at the airport and drives you to the town of Te Anau, which is across the lake from Fiordland.

While your uncle and his friend, Murdoch, study their maps, you are sent to buy supplies. You pack the knapsack carefully. Canned beans, beef jerky, chocolate chip cookies, coffee, a flashlight—all the things you will need for your stay in Fiordland.

That night in the campground, your uncle shows you pictures of the artifacts that he and Murdoch will be seeking: moa-egg water bottles, weapons, jewelry made from sharks' teeth.

"We might even find some skeletal remains," he adds. "Wouldn't that be something?"

"What if we found the Lost Tribe?" you ask casually.

Charlie grins. "The Tribe no longer exists," he says. "Get some sleep. We want to get an early start."

You curl up in your sleeping bag with one of his books about the Maoris and read by flashlight for a long time. When you get too tired to read, you search the sky for the Southern Cross. You don't find it, but you do see a beautiful bright star fall from the heavens to the dark waters of the lake. Perhaps it's an omen.

Finally you fall asleep.

Turn to page 7.

You head downstream. If the boy is trying to hide from you, the thick foliage will give him good cover. Soon the undergrowth at the river's edge becomes so thick that you can no longer push through it.

You hop to an island in the middle of the stream. You're determined to find that boy. What if he's from the Lost Tribe?

A rumbling noise makes you look up. It can't be thunder! The sky is blue. But wait. Off toward the mountains something is glowing. Is it a forest fire? The mountain starts to shake. The ground beneath your feet trembles. The sky hazes over.

It's a volcano! And it's erupting! Soft gray ashes float down on you. You run, splashing in the shallow water, as the stream of molten lava cascades down the riverbed. You round a bend and see a band of men—perhaps thirty of them—ahead of you. They're Maori warriors! The boy is riding on the back of one, and another is carrying the dog!

"Wait!" you yell. *"Wait!"*

One of the huge men scoops you up in his arms and carries you like a small child. His long powerful legs race down the riverbed. But the stream of boiling lava runs faster than all of you.

You have found the Lost Tribe. But no one will ever know.

The End

In the morning, you cross Lake Te Anau in a rented motor boat and dock at a rickety pier. The heavy foliage of Fiordland comes right down to the water's edge. You are unloading the supplies when your uncle throws up his hands. "I don't believe it!" he groans. "I've got our permit, I've got the maps—but I left the shovels and sifting gear in the trunk of the car!"

Your uncle has never been known for his good memory. Sometimes your birthday cards come six months late.

"I'll stay here and set up camp," you say. "You and Murdoch go back for the gear."

"Well . . ." Charlie says, frowning. You know he is worried about leaving you alone. "Put this permit in your pocket in case the ranger comes by. Fiordland is a restricted area."

"Let's go," says Murdoch impatiently. "We're wasting time!"

You watch until the motorboat becomes a small speck on the lake.

You could set up camp as you promised. But you could also start exploring—right now!

*If you decide to explore,
turn to page 9.*

*If you decide to set up camp,
turn to page 11.*

You decide you'll have plenty of time to set up camp before Charlie and Murdoch get back. With mounting excitement, you start off through the forest. The crunching noise of your footsteps echoes in nature's quiet.

A low growl penetrates the calm. You stop and duck down in the brush. A brown-skinned boy about your own age is coming toward you. He has Maori features, but he's not dressed like the young Maoris you saw on the streets of Te Anau, who wore blue jeans and T-shirts. This boy is wearing a knee-length skirt of reeds. Attached to his belt are two gray ducks, and sharks' teeth hang from rings in his ears.

A soft-coated white dog trots behind him.

You lie very still. Should you speak to him or hide until he passes and then follow him? He might lead you to the Lost Tribe!

*If you speak to the boy,
turn to page 26.*

*If you stay in hiding,
turn to page 12.*

10

The Maori scouts leave the tunnel in a few minutes, carrying the injured hunter.

They are so intent on getting him back to the village that they don't notice you slipping away as they cross the meadow. This time you find the right tunnel quickly. Within an hour you are back at the campsite with your uncle and Murdoch.

They are impressed with your red kaka feathers and ask you to show them the place in the forest where you found them.

Fortunately, it is stormy the next day. The day after that, they forget about the feathers when Murdoch finds a bone barb from a hunting spear.

You could tell them where to find two more of those, but you don't—because they'd never believe you.

The End

You unpack the gear in a clearing a few hundred feet from the lake. The forest is eerily quiet, and you wonder if any wild animals live in this overgrown area. You are setting up camp when you hear a rustling noise behind you. Could it be the ranger?

You whirl around. A skinny brown dog springs from the bushes and knocks you to the ground. A dark-skinned young man moves out of the shrubbery toward you. He is wearing cut-off jeans and no shirt.

He scowls and spits on the ground.

"Pakeha!" he says scornfully. "White one!" He waves a short-handled tomahawk at you.

He's about the same height as you are, but his build is very muscular.

He pushes the dog away and yanks you to your feet. He rips a vine from the ground and ties your hands behind your back.

"Come!" he snarls.

Turn to page 25.

12

You stay in hiding as the Maori boy passes by. But the white dog senses your presence and veers toward you. Immediately the boy snaps his fingers, and the dog backs off. As you watch, you remember an illustration in the book you were reading last night. It showed a dog that looked just like this one.

But the book said that the breed was extinct!

Your mind is racing! Could the Lost Tribe really exist?

You crawl from your hiding place, your feet squishing in the damp soil. You step to one side—hoping to avoid the marsh—and sink to your ankles. Your feet become tangled in something. Vines? No! It's a series of nooses!

You are struggling to free yourself when you hear a noise. You turn and stare up into the tattooed face of a Maori hunter. He is easily six and a half feet tall. He reaches down. With one swift motion, he cuts through the snare with a small, pointed stone dagger.

"Come," he says sternly.

You glance across the narrow marsh. You're sure it's a shortcut back to the lake. This is scary. Do you really want to find the Tribe? Or should you run while you have the chance?

If you decide to run, turn to page 58.

If you decide to follow the hunter, turn to page 57.

Followed by the dog, you skirt the edge of the meadow, stealthily probing the underbrush until you find the right opening.

Just as you drop to your knees to enter, the dog growls. You turn. Something is moving in the meadow!

Something that is ten feet tall!

The monster gnaws at the grass as it moves clumsily toward you. It comes closer, and you see that it's a gigantic bird with huge heavy legs—much bigger than yours. But its wings are only tiny little flaps.

Can it be? It is!

It's the legendary moa—a flightless bird that has been extinct for centuries! You saw a moa skeleton in the Auckland museum the last time you visited your uncle.

You duck quickly into the tunnel.

Turn to page 15.

14

You open your hand and drop the keys into the waters of the glacier-gouged lake. Babyface lunges for you, but not fast enough. He swings at you, cursing—but you step aside, and his hand crashes into the metal deck rail.

"I'll kill you for that!" he snaps.

"Cut me loose," says your uncle. "I'll hot-wire it for you."

You stare at him, incredulous. Has he lost his mind?

"Cut him loose," says one convict. "We've got to get out of here before the ranger shows up."

The other man reluctantly cuts the ropes tying your uncle and Murdoch together.

"Cut this one loose, too," says Babyface, pointing to you. "I'm starving. All I've eaten for three days is berries."

He shoves you toward the tiny kitchen. "Fix us something to eat," he orders you. "And no tricks!"

"Would I trick you?" you mutter.

Turn to page 70.

You and the dog hurry through the tunnel. It widens and gets higher and you're sure that it's the one leading back to the forest. You make your way through the underbrush and skirt the marsh. Finally you see the light of the campfire by the lake.

Uncle Charlie rushes out to meet you and gives you a bearhug. Then he gasps.

"The dog," he says. "Where did you find that dog?" His voice drops to a whisper. "That breed has been extinct for two hundred years!"

You tell him and Murdoch your story, and they plan excitedly to retrace your steps at dawn.

But when you lead them into the forest, you are unable to find the original trail. You spend three days looking for the pa of the Lost Tribe without success. Finally bad weather stops your search entirely. During the night of the third day, the dog disappears.

Every year for a decade after that, your uncle takes a group of archeologists into the rain forest by Lake Te Anau. But he never finds the Tribe.

You are the only one who succeeded at that.

The End

Grasping the heavy chunk of greenstone, you creep back to the clearing. One man has been left to guard your uncle Charlie and Murdoch.

You take aim. The greenstone arches into the air, cracks him on the temple, and knocks him unconscious.

"Good work," says your uncle proudly as you untie him. Together the two of you tie the guard's hands behind his back.

"Who are they?" you ask.

"They're escaped convicts," he answers. "They're stealing greenstone from the national parklands to finance their way to North America. They damaged their boat coming in, and they need our launch to get themselves and their haul out of here."

"Who's the boy?" you ask.

"He's no boy," Charlie replies. "He's Babyface Tioko, notorious armed robber. His picture was in last Sunday's paper."

You lead the guard back through the forest to Lake Te Anau, where you board your launch and cross over to town. The police chief sends some officers back to round up the other two convicts.

The next day, when your uncle and Murdoch go back to look for artifacts, you decide not to join them. Instead you go trout fishing on Lake Te Anau.

The End

You have an advantage over the Maori duck hunters who are pursuing you. They're still in the marsh. You're already out of the water and free of the mud. You crash through the forest toward your uncle's camp. You don't even look back. You know the hunters will come only so far and then stop.

If they are seen by other white men, the Lost Tribe will be discovered.

You reach camp—out of breath, filthy, and wet.

Uncle Charlie is mad at you for ruining your clothes. When you try to explain, he accuses you of making up stories. You spend the rest of the afternoon sunning by Lake Te Anau.

That night, around the campfire, your uncle tells how the Maoris used to hunt for ducks by submerging themselves in a marsh and camouflaging their heads with tufts of flax.

You stifle a yawn and try to look interested. The truth is, despite all your uncle's schooling, you know more about it than he does.

The End

You get down on your hands and knees and lower yourself over the ledge, searching for toe-holds. Suddenly you lose your grip on the rock wall. You slide straight down at a terrifying pace, until, with a thump, you are stopped by a small shelf. The sound of rushing water is getting louder.

You slide on your stomach, feet first, for the last thirty feet and plunge into the raging icy water. You're powerless against this channel's tantrums. And the deafening thunder, echoing through the cathedrallike cavern, can mean only one thing.

You're going over the falls.

Like a rag doll, you're tossed and thrown—down, down—pummeled sideways, head first, feet first—down to the fast-flowing river hundreds of feet below.

By some miracle, it is not the end. When you regain consciousness, you are out in the forest. Above you twinkles the Southern Cross. Around you are people with torches. Beside you is a shallow, swift-flowing river.

Your uncle's face comes into focus. You try to sit up, but the pain is too great.

Turn to page 67.

You duck back into the tunnel. Wind whips the needlelike rain in at you, and you huddle close to the wall for protection. As you squat there, chilled and hungry, you hear a strange crackling sound above the noise of the storm. Then a thundering roar. But it's not thunder. You look up.

Part of the mountain is breaking away! Rocks and ice, crash down the steep slope, stopping abruptly right over the entrance to the cave.

You lean against the wall, trembling at the thought of your close call. That's when you hear it—the sound of breathing.

There is someone in the tunnel behind you.

Cautiously you turn. Two glowing amber lights are approaching. A bark rips through the darkness—and the white dog from the pa scampers toward you, tail wagging.

You sigh and sit down on the rock floor to think. The dog ambles over and lays his head in your lap. You decide to wait until dark to go back and find the right tunnel.

You doze off. When you wake up there are stars overhead. The storm has moved out to sea. It is time to go.

You retrace your steps. The dog follows. At the other end of the tunnel, you peer across the meadow toward the pa. There is no activity. The village is asleep.

Turn to page 13.

You jump into the trench, slipping and sliding in the soft dirt. Anxiously you look behind you. No one is following. As you turn a corner, you realize that this is no simple trench, but a network of ditches for protection of the village.

Ahead of you there is a two-pronged fork. One path must lead to the meadow, but which one?

If you choose the right fork,
turn to page 48.

If you choose the left fork,
turn to page 81.

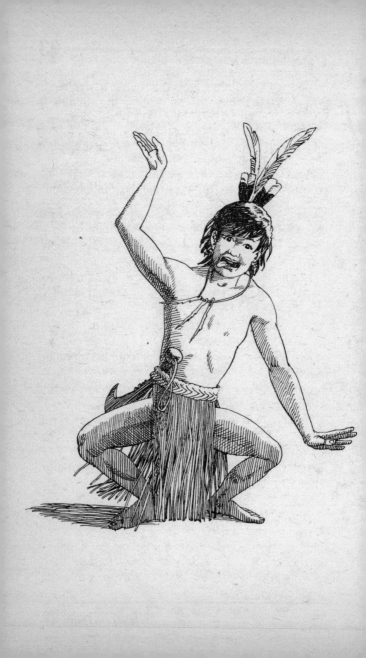

You trust Hohepa, so you follow as he leads you to the *marae*—the square by the gate. It is brightly lit with torches held by the villagers.

The tribe's spear thrower enters, followed by rows of skirted warriors in battle regalia. Hohepa joins the warriors.

At a motion from the Ariki, they spring into ferocious action, grimacing and leaping—roaring out an ancient war chant. When the performance ends, they thrust out their weapons and jump—landing full-footed on the dirt with an earth-shaking thud.

The Tohunga steps forward and draws a three-pronged fork in the dirt with the rakau whakapapa.

"Whetu," he intones, looking at you.

"Whetu," the people chant.

The Tohunga erases two prongs of the drawing with his bare foot, leaving only the longest line—the one in the middle. You know this represents the third test, and your heart pounds.

Hohepa leaps in front of you. His eyes roll wildly, and his tongue hangs from his mouth. This is the Maori invitation to battle.

This raging youth—is he the same person who shared his dinner with you?

Turn to page 72.

Stepping gingerly on the ledge, you feel along the wall with your hands. You know that at any second the narrow rock shelf could vanish into the black void beside you and send you hurtling to the bottom of the chasm.

You try your flashlight, but the batteries are dead.

Another bat brushes up against you. You jerk back in surprise, almost losing your balance. You stop to calm your jittery nerves and squint into the darkness. Beside you, on the rock wall, you notice greenish-white flecks glowing in the dark.

Could it be moonlight? Phosphorus in the rock?

You move along as quickly as you dare, ducking down as the ledge turns into a cave—a breathtaking cave, shimmering with muted light. The walls and ceiling are dotted with millions of tiny stars—pinpricks that glow like miniature fluorescent lights.

Speechless, you stand and stare.

You have found the Glowing Caves!

Turn to page 98.

The dog growls at your heels as the young man in cutoffs pushes you deeper into the forest. You walk for almost an hour—crawling up rocky inclines and thrashing through thickets, sometimes doubling back, sometimes going forward. At times you think your captor has lost his way. Finally you come to a clearing. Two men stand at the far side watching you approach.

"What took you so long?" shouts one. "We got ours the minute they docked!"

Startled at his words, you look across the clearing. At the edge of the forest, tied together, stand Murdoch and your uncle Charlie.

"We've got their boat," the man continues. "But we can't kill them here."

Your mind races. Whoever these people are, they mean business! Your uncle and Murdoch can't run. It's up to you. But your hands are tied, and it's three against one.

Still, you might have a chance.

If you decide to run,
turn to page 42.

If you decide that escape is impossible,
turn to page 64.

You jump from your hiding place as the Maori boy passes.

"Wait!" you cry out.

The boy whirls around and, like a frightened deer, darts into the forest.

You hear one sharp whistle. In an instant, the dog is gone—vanishing into the heavy foliage after his master.

"Hey!" you yell. "Wait!"

But the only reply is a parrot crying out its Maori name. "Kaka . . . kaka . . . kaka . . ."

You scramble to your feet and thrash into the underbrush after them. You go for several hundred yards and reach a wide riverbed. Only a trickle of water runs over the gravel. In some places, the bed rises above the water, forming small islands.

Which way did he go? To the left, toward the mountains—or downstream, where the river disappears into a thicket?

*If you go toward the mountains,
turn to page 28.*

*If you follow the river downstream,
turn to page 5.*

A villager shouts as you lead the scouts carrying the stretcher from the tunnel toward the pa. The Ariki rushes out, runs to the injured man's side, and embraces him.

You have saved the brother of the tribal chief!

A feast is prepared in your honor. You are served roast parrot and oysters fried in shark oil. The villagers perform poi dances and tangi songs. Everyone joins in the celebration except one warrior whom you notice standing alone in the shadows. He makes you a little uneasy.

When the feast ends, the Ariki calls for silence.

"What is your desire?" he asks you.

"To return to my people," you answer.

The Ariki's clear brown eyes study you.

"Like pigeons of the valley," he says, nodding, "the wise ones return to the nurturing nest."

At his words, the solitary warrior strikes his spear fiercely on the ground and leaps forward.

"One fish will lead the school to the net!" he says angrily.

"But the secret of the Lost Tribe is safe with me!" you protest.

The Ariki claps his hands for order. "The Council will bring you word at dawn," he says to you.

You're taken back to the House of Gold and locked in. Should you trust the Tribal Council to make a fair decision? Or should you dig your way out of here again?

If you decide to wait, turn to page 73.

If you decide to dig your way out, turn to page 96.

You head toward the mountains, hopping from island to island in the river—and sometimes halting to skip a pebble out into the shallow icy water.

Suddenly you stop. A slim brown-skinned woman is standing on one of the islands. She is dressed in a skirt of flax. Three red kaka feathers are fastened in her long black hair.

She turns as you approach. Her lips and the skin under her mouth are heavily tattooed, just like the pictures of the ancient Maoris in the book your uncle gave you.

She beckons you to come closer. As you approach, you see that she has been crying.

"Is something wrong?" you ask.

"Death flirts with my father, the Tohunga," she replies.

Your uncle told you about the Tohungas—the tribal priests.

"I beg the gods to sharpen my gift of second sight, so I may know his future," she says. She looks skyward. "It is good that you did not follow the river to the thicket," she continues, "for trouble awaits you there."

How did she know you were thinking of going downstream? A spooky feeling comes over you. Maybe you should get back to the lake and see if your uncle and Murdoch have returned.

If you shake off the spooky feeling and stay, turn to page 74.

If you decide to go back to the lake, turn to page 37.

You decide that you should stay under the House of Gold. You crawl to the building's edge to breathe some fresh air. Through a crack you can see an unattended *hangi*—an earth oven— steaming the evening meal. The hangi is beside a small building, and the cries of a child inside make you suspect that this is a villager's home.

You squint through the crack again. Is that really steam? No! It's smoke! The villager's house is on fire!

The child is screaming now, but no one comes. The Maoris are all out looking for you!

You must do something. Clawing frantically at the soft ground, you squeeze out from under the house. You race to the doorway. The terrified child is in a corner.

You rush in, snatch her up, and run outside— crashing headfirst into an ornately dressed man whose skin is painted red.

Only the chief—the Ariki—wears red ocher. You read that last night. His face shows neither pleasure nor anger.

The others are off looking for you. This man is alone. Should you risk an escape now, or should you try to reason with him? You might never find your way back without a guide.

If you decide to run, turn to page 115.

If you ask the Ariki for a guide to take you back to the lake, turn to page 53.

You grab the sapling and hope you remember everything your coach ever taught you about pole vaulting.

You push down hard, propelling yourself up—up—up into the air, over the tall wooden barricade that rings the village. You land in a clump of soft ferns on the forest floor.

An appreciative chorus of "ahs" comes from inside the pa. Then the dancing and the music become more intense. Smiling to yourself, you run through the forest.

Your uncle Charlie is upset about your disappearance. His attitude is what makes you decide. The location of the Lost Tribe will remain your secret forever. Let the archeologists keep their little chunks of greenstone. You don't want them interfering with the lives of Wiremu's happy people.

Years later, after you have established your medical practice in the United States, you take your family to New Zealand for a visit.

Your uncle tells you of a new Maori legend he has heard . . . not of glowing caves or caves of rushing water, but of a flying white being who breathed life into a drowning child.

You smile and wonder what ever happened to Wiremu.

The End

You bolt for the cave, splashing through shallow pools on the ledge. From your sheltered spot, you look out at the mountains beyond. They are laced with ribbons of white. Waterfalls—dozens, maybe hundreds—have been primed by the sudden storm.

You move farther into the cave. A rough passageway seems to lead to another cavern. The rock walls are covered with strange pictures. One drawing, in rust-covered paint, shows a serpent rising from the sea. Another is scratched into the rock. It's a sketch of the giant moa—the extinct flightless bird. You saw one in the book your uncle gave you.

You move toward the passageway and stop. Two long slender spears with barbed bone tips are leaning against the rock wall.

Your heart pounds. These are not artifacts. No hunter would abandon a weapon. The owners must be in the cavern beyond!

You must return to the tunnel before you're discovered.

You are moving toward the entrance when you hear a rumble. The cave shakes under your feet.

Earthquake? No.

Avalanche!

Can you risk running for the tunnel now? At least you can get back to the meadow from there.

If you run for the tunnel,
turn to page 51.

If you stay in the cave,
turn to page 75.

The totara trunk is obviously the central pillar for a building. But where is the sacrifice for the gods?

You're smart. You can figure it out.

You're dealing with an ancient tribe. They won't use a block of greenstone. They want you.

When the warrior swings his stone mere, you never know what hits you.

Your disappearance in the forest by Lake Te Anau is just as big a mystery to your family as the Lost Tribe of Fiordland was to you.

The End

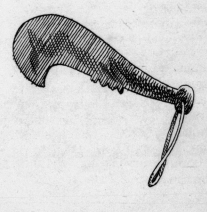

34

Your heart pounds as you creep down the stairs into a dark, cluttered room. You trip over a carved wooden *tiki*. Your uncle explained about the tiki to you earlier. It represents the Maori idea of the first human being. Many people think tikis are good luck symbols. You've seen hundreds in New Zealand, from tiny ones on key rings to massive ones on buildings.

But you've never seen one like this. This tiki stares blankly up from the floor. The eyes, which are usually greenstone or abalone shell, are missing.

You shudder and look around. There are seven tikis in the room—all with their eyes removed!

Something white over in a corner catches your attention. You gasp in horror. It's a pile of bones! You count five . . . six . . . seven skulls!

A strange double tiki is mounted on the wall above the bones. It looks like Siamese twins joined at the feet. The upper tiki is carved in greenstone. The lower one, hanging upside-down, is fashioned in gold.

Why would they leave a treasure like that down here? What does it mean? And where did those bones come from?

A noise overhead startles you. You run to the stairs.

Turn to page 85.

You stay in a half-crouch, stunned by the lights in the cave and terrorized by the warriors. Far back in the cavern, on a ledge above the warriors' heads, sit the Tohunga and the small boy who almost drowned.

The Tohunga points the tribal stick accusingly at you and speaks in a voice like thunder.

"The timid one runs like a dog from his duty!"

He glares at you and lays one hand protectively on the head of the little boy.

You get the point. They still think you have special powers and are angry because you did not help the boy.

You are still crouched in the entrance to the tunnel. The nearest warrior is twenty feet away. Could you possibly escape?

If you decide to back out of the cavern and run, turn to page 107.

If you decide that running would be useless, turn to page 110.

"Well, I'd better get back to the lake now," you say to the woman. You try to sound casual. "My uncle will be worried."

You run until you reach the place where the river flows into the thicket. Her words come back to you.

"For trouble awaits you there . . ."

You frown. That's superstitious! The boy and his dog must have come this way, and you'd really like to find them.

The riverbed narrows as it leads into the thicket. You scramble for shore as the water gets deeper. The heavy foliage blots out the daylight and you push through, looking for a trail. You're about to give up and go back when you come to the edge of a small grove.

You have found the boy! But he is captive—tied to a sapling—and three wild-looking Maori hunters are threatening him! One stands menacingly over him, a leather thong wrapped around his hand.

Should you try to stop them yourself, or should you get your uncle and Murdoch?

*If you run back to the lake for help,
turn to page 44.*

*If you decide to stop the hunters on your own,
turn to page 105.*

38

You don't want to be trapped. You suppress your curiosity and carefully replace the section of the floor just as Wiremu returns. To your dismay, he is empty-handed.

"Food?" you say, hesitantly.

"Not here," he whispers. "Sacred place. *Tapu.*"

He leads you out of the carved house and around to the back of the building. On the ground are a wooden bowl of steaming soup and a chunk of bread wrapped in a large leaf.

You sit leaning up against the building and eagerly drink from the bowl, picking out chunks of meat with your fingers.

Wiremu stands guard as you wolf down the food. Suddenly a furious wailing erupts from the center of the pa. Feet pound on the dirt as the villagers race toward the noise. Two warriors run past without noticing you.

Wiremu cranes his neck. You shove the bread into your pocket and stand up so you can see, too. There is so much confusion that you're sure you won't be noticed.

You grab Wiremu's arm. "Let's go!" you say.

Turn to page 99.

Villagers follow you along the dirt streets until the Tohunga stops at the entrance to a carved meeting house. He pushes open a sliding door and motions for you to enter. As you do, you are dazzled by a bright glow at the rear of the room. The back wall is completely covered with hammered gold!

Go on to the next page.

40

The building is full of gold! Gold nuggets are heaped into chests. Rocks with heavy veins of gold exposed line the walls. An altar at one end of the room is studded with chunks of the precious metal.

What is this?
You whirl around just in time to see the door sliding shut.

Turn to page 43.

You remember seeing a fern-covered gully near the clearing. If you can reach that, you may be able to hide there until you can cut your hands free.

Your uncle Charlie is staring at you. You nod your head twice, very slowly. It's the "steal" signal you used to use when he was coaching your softball team back home. He gets the point immediately. He lets out a wild whoop and lurches forward, dragging Murdoch down with him.

Murdoch yells in surprise. Your captor runs to investigate—and you dart into the forest. You reach the gully and tumble in. Pounding feet go by on the trail above.

But you have forgotten one thing. The dog has picked up your scent! You hear a growl—and then he crashes down the side of the gully.

Quickly you rub your bindings on a sharp rock. As the dog leaps toward you, the vine breaks. You snatch a piece of beef jerky from your pocket and throw it to him. He drops to his belly and chews the treat eagerly.

Now you must get back to Charlie and Murdoch. But you'd better arm yourself first. You grab a rock . . . and then let out a low whistle. The rock isn't granite. It's greenstone! The gully is full of precious greenstone!

Turn to page 16.

"No!" you yell. You try to force the heavy panel open.

It's locked! You are captive in a house of gold.

But why? Are these Maoris friendly or hostile? Should you wait to see what the Tribe is going to do with you? Or should you try to escape?

*If you decide to wait and see,
turn to page 71.*

*If you decide to try to escape,
turn to page 78.*

You're no match for three Maori hunters. You must hurry!

Your uncle Charlie and Murdoch should be back by now. You run through the brambles, your heart pounding. Will you make it in time to help the boy?

You come out of the thicket on the edge of a chasm—and your heart sinks. You must have taken a wrong turn. The river is twenty feet below you. There's no time to climb down and back up the other side.

The distance across the gorge is only about six feet. You have no choice. You *must* jump it!

You back up. With a running leap you hurtle across the gap.

You make it across! But the ground on the other side crumbles under your weight. You drop into the churning white water below.

You'll never know what happened to the boy and his dog. And your uncle and Murdoch will never solve the mystery of your disappearance.

The woman was right. Trouble awaited you.

The End

You push through the undergrowth, looking for a trail the woman might have taken. The sand flies are a nuisance, and you become frustrated and tired. Just as you decide to abandon your search, the sky rumbles ominously.

You look up. The sheet of blue that stretched overhead all morning has been replaced with black thunderheads.

You must hurry back to the campsite!

Cold, sudden rain pours down on you, whipping your face and drenching your clothes. You run to the riverbed and stare with horror at what faces you. The placid, trickling river has been transformed into a torrent of raging water!

Frantic, you wade in. You have to get across before it becomes impassable.

But the river has a mind of its own. It picks you up and drags you downstream, like a spinning leaf. At last it leaves you on a bank deep in the rain forest.

You wander for days. When you are finally found, you babble to your rescuers about a woman's father and visions.

Your withered mind is incapable of logical thought. In your own sad way, you are as lost as the legendary Lost Tribe.

The End

The Tohunga holds up his hand, and the crowd becomes silent. Solemnly he approaches you. When he reaches the base of the chair, he bows low and hands you the tribe's rakau whaka-papa! The villagers follow after him. Each person lays a gift at the foot of your perch.

Gold nuggets, greenstone, hunting knives, carved objects, sharks' teeth—all are piled up at your feet. But the final offering is the most startling.

The last person in line is the mother of the child you saved. And her gift is the boy! You have often joked at home about wanting a slave, but this is too much!

You find Wiremu in the crowd and beckon to him. It is already dusk. You must put an end to this. You reach for the flashlight in your pocket and start to plan.

Go on to the next page.

You gesture that you want to come down. Wiremu turns to one of the men, and a beautifully carved ladder is quickly leaned up against the thronelike chair.

You scramble down. Putting on your most serious expression, you shine the flashlight on the dark hair of the child.

The villagers gasp and back away. The boy's mother cries out. You pick up the youngster and carry him to his grateful mother's arms. Then— hoping you return the right gift to the right person—you shine your light on each treasure as you give them all back. Bowing low, you hand the tribal stick to the Tohunga.

There is only one thing left.

You walk to Wiremu and place your floral crown on his head. Then, holding the flashlight in front of you, you walk backward out through the double gates, back into the real world—your world. You hope that the Lost Tribe will never be found again.

The last thing you see before you turn to run through the forest is Wiremu, perched high in the lofty chair.

The End

48

You take the right fork in the trench.

The high dirt walls that tower over you magnify the thudding sound of your running feet. You reach another fork and continue on to the right, thinking about the tremendous amount of manual labor that went into building the trenches. The Tribe certainly hasn't heard about bulldozers! Once more, in the maze of passageways, you veer to the right. You hope that you are working your way toward the meadow.

Perspiring, dirty, panting for breath, you slow down. Ahead of you, the channel narrows and turns. You see grass on the upper edges. The meadow! You've made it!

Turn to page 116.

50

You clench the keys tightly in your hand.

"The kid has the keys," says your uncle, nodding at you.

Babyface leaps at you, wrenches open your fingers, and tosses the key ring to one of the convicts. Your uncle winks at you and grins. Murdoch looks puzzled. You scowl. Is your uncle crazy?

One convict effortlessly starts up the launch. But less than a mile down the fiord, the motor sputters, chugs, and stops. Now you understand! Murdoch grins. He understands too. Your forgetful uncle forgot to buy gas when he went back to town. He knew they wouldn't get far!

"There's a ranger's storehouse about a mile inland," says your uncle. "There might be some gas there."

"Check it out," one of the men says to Babyface. "And take the kid with you."

They untie your hands. You and Babyface inflate a rubber raft and paddle to the bank. You push your way through the undergrowth, swatting and scratching at sand flies.

"There it is! I see it!" Babyface yells.

Before you can stop him, he starts through a patch of waist-high speargrass. Then he runs back into the clearing, yelling with pain, his bare legs covered with bleeding slashes.

"I'm bleeding to death," he whines.

"Bleeding isn't the problem," you say. "I read all about speargrass. It's poison! I'll go look for the gas and figure out some way to get you back to the boat. Lie down and keep still."

Turn to page 106.

You race from the cave and dive into the tunnel, panting. The side of the mountain trembles as the avalanche advances down the slope.

Suddenly, at the cave's entrance, you see a figure. Two figures! The Maori hunters!

"Run!" you scream, but your voice is swallowed by the storm.

One hunter is almost clear of the cave when the slide slams into the ledge. Clutching his spear, he is bounced like a toy and carried down to the valley below.

You crawl across the ledge to reach the second Maori. His legs are pinned under rocks and ice, but he is alive. Using a tree limb as a crowbar and digging with your hands, you are able to free him. You drag him into the shelter of the tunnel.

He is semiconscious and in terrible pain. One of his legs is crushed. You must get help. But how?

If you return to the pa alone, the Tribe will kill you before you can tell them about their comrade. And taking him back through the tunnel seems almost impossible.

If you take your chances on going back to the pa alone, turn to page 95.

If you decide to move the hunter through the tunnel, turn to page 92.

"I need help to get back to the lake," you say to the Ariki.

"Whetu," says the Ariki, taking the child from you.

Immediately you are seized from behind by two warriors. Your feet and hands are bound with vines and you are carried to a small hut beside the House of Gold. The villagers follow, cheering.

This time you are not left alone. A young Maori is assigned to guard you. You sit on the floor and stare at him.

"What's your name?" you ask.

"Hohepa," he replies.

"Why won't they let me go, Hohepa?"

He toys with the tomahawk on his belt before he answers. "It is the star in the prophecy," he says softly. "Many harvests ago, our chief had a vision that when the star, whetu, fell to Lake Te Anau, one would come unwilling to the Tribe. This promised one, whom the Chief named *Whetu* for the star, would lead us to victory over the pakeha—the white man—and would restore to us our lands."

Your mind flashes back to the falling star you saw last night.

"If they think I'm Whetu," you say, "why am I tied up?"

"There are three tests," says Hohepa. "You have passed only two."

Puzzled, you think for a moment. "The rescue. That was a test, wasn't it? The fire was a fake. Only smoke."

Hohepa nods.

Turn to page 97.

You hurry across the riverbed and back to the campsite. Excitedly you tell your uncle Charlie and Murdoch about the woman.

They exchange glances and press you for details. Finally they ask you to lead them to the spot where you saw her.

As you tramp through the forest, thunder rumbles overhead, and a sudden downpour drenches you. When you reach the riverbed, you find a wild torrent of water rushing down to the sea. The island where she stood has disappeared.

On the way back, Charlie and Murdoch tell you the legend of Meriana, daughter of an eighteenth-century Tohunga, known throughout the island for her gift of *mata-kite*—second sight.

As you leave the forest, you stoop to pick up something on the trail: three red kaka feathers, fastened with a ring of bone.

When the storm subsides, the three of you decide to return to Te Anau for the night, since your campground is flooded. A rainbow follows you all the way across the lake.

The End

You must distract this mob. With one quick movement you thrust the torch into the heap of dry grass. There is a bright flash as the mound erupts into a giant bonfire that ignites the palisade around the pa. Pandemonium breaks out.

You sprint for the gates, your feet pounding on the soft dirt. Across the clearing and into the forest you run, panting hard. You look back. The pa is ringed by a wall of fire.

You reach a river and splash through the shallow cold water, not thinking about where you are or where you're going. Escape is uppermost in your mind. You know they would have killed you. You know you've failed the third test.

But you couldn't have killed Hohepa. No way!

You push on until you have no strength left. Then you curl up on a bed of moss and sleep.

You wander for many days. When you are finally found, you are flown home and hospitalized. It takes weeks for your mind and body to heal from your days of deprivation in the rain forest. Your family and your doctors think you are hallucinating when you try to tell them about your adventures.

Years later, when your first son is born, you name him Joseph. But you always call him by his Maori name—Hohepa.

The End

What a strange woman! You decide to continue your search for the boy and his dog.

"I have to go now," you say, backing away.

She does not seem to hear you.

She kneels and presses her head to the gravel on the tiny island. It occurs to you that the mound looks like a burial site.

Her low voice carries on the breeze as she chants.

"Wait for me here, father! It's only a shower."

You puzzle over this. Overhead, the sky is light blue. The only clouds you see are far out over the mountains. You swat at a sand fly, and when you look up, the woman has vanished.

It's not possible! Something weird is happening here!

Forget about looking for the boy. You'd better get back to the lake!

Turn to page 54.

You follow the hunter as he moves silently through the heavy undergrowth.

Why run? you think. You came to find the Tribe! This is an adventure! Not until you feel cold air on your face do you realize that you've been led into an underground tunnel. Water trickles down the rock walls, and you have to crouch as the passageway gets lower and narrower and darker.

You think you must be inside the Murchison Range. The water must be coming from snow-fed glaciers above. What if there were an earthquake while you were in here?

You decide to go back and turn to leave. But that's impossible! Another fierce Maori is silently following you. There is no escape now.

Abruptly the glare of sunlight blinds you. You crawl from the tunnel into a mountain meadow. You look up, blinking. You are surrounded by Maori warriors. They are brandishing spears.

Turn to page 59.

There could be unknown risks if you follow the hunter. You don't want to chance it.

Mud sucks at your feet as you turn and run clumsily through the marsh, scattering a few noisy ducks. When you reach solid ground, you turn, expecting to see the hunter following. But he has disappeared!

Instead of relief, you feel disappointment. If the hunter and the boy *were* members of the Lost Tribe, you know you'll never see them again.

You go back to the shore of Lake Te Anau and start setting up camp.

You've blown your chance. The Tribe will go into hiding now until you and your uncle and Murdoch leave. You'll never find the Lost Tribe. You'll have to settle for artifacts.

The End

Beyond the warriors, you see a *pa*, a native village with a stockade and trench around the perimeter. The sound of voices and the cry of a baby from inside tell you what you have already guessed.

The Lost Tribe of Fiordland exists.

Turn to page 61.

The largest warrior in the circle raises his spear. His tongue is hanging lopsidedly from his mouth in the Maori sign for battle, and his dark eyes flash wildly. The straight blue tattoo lines on his face—his *moko*—are grotesque. He is the fiercest-looking person you have ever seen.

Turn to page 63.

62

You dash across the mountain meadow without looking back once. You duck into the first opening you see. Glaciers have carved many tunnels and caves into this rocky terrain, and you can only hope that this one is a tunnel that leads back to the forest by the lake.

The passageway is much longer than the one through which the hunter brought you. It's colder, too, and you seem to be climbing uphill.

You exit on a rocky plateau high up on the side of the mountain. The sky grumbles threateningly and drops a sudden sheet of rain.

Discouraged and disappointed, you look for shelter. There is another opening on the ledge over to your left. It looks like a cave, but it might be a tunnel. Perhaps it's a passageway out to the forest by Lake Te Anau.

But maybe you should just wait out the storm. The rain is whipping into the tunnel. Would the cave give you more protection?

If you stay in the tunnel, turn to page 20.

If you seek shelter in the cave, turn to page 32.

The warrior is leaning back on one leg to hurl the spear at you when the white dog that you saw on the trail comes running out of the pa, directly to you. He licks your feet and playfully jumps up.

The dog seems to distract the warriors. Maybe you can make it back to the tunnel. They can't throw spears in there!

If you run for the tunnel, turn to page 82.

If you decide running would mean certain death, turn to page 91.

64

"Let's go!" says your captor gruffly, pushing you over to where your uncle and Murdoch are standing. "Come on! Move it!" He heads out of the clearing. The rest of you follow.

"Who are they?" you whisper to your uncle.

"Convicts," he whispers back. "Escaped from the Auckland prison. Their pictures were in all the newspapers."

"But what about the boy?" you ask.

"He's no boy," says your uncle. "He's Baby-face Tioko—one of the most ruthless crooks in New Zealand."

"What do they want with us?"

Your uncle smiles. "Our launch. They rammed theirs into the rocks trying to get out to the sea last night. They think they can reach open water on the middle fiord." He leans closer and lowers his voice even more. "Do you still have the spare set of keys I gave you? I dropped mine over the side when they came on board."

You nod as they herd you onto the boat.

You slip your bound hands into your back pocket while the convicts frisk your uncle and Murdoch. Just as your finger latches on to the metal ring, Babyface shouts and points at you. Your back is to the water.

Think fast! Will your lives be in more danger if you drop the keys overboard—or will you be buying time to escape?

If you decide to drop the keys, turn to page 14.

If you decide it's safer not to drop them,
turn to page 50.

You move away from Wiremu and inch toward the gates. The Tohunga has reached the mother and child. He takes the little boy from her and, holding the youngster like a rag doll in front of him, squeezes his midriff—in and out, in and out.

You feel as if everything is going to be okay.

Relieved, you sprint for the forest. As you thrash through the scrub, a child's cry reaches your ears, and then the sounds of rejoicing from inside the pa. The little boy is all right!

You hurry to the tunnel opening and crawl through. You've gone several hundred yards when you realize that the tunnel seems different. It's wider and higher!

When you come to a fork, you know that what you suspected is true. You are in a different passageway.

If you take the left fork, turn to page 102.

If you take the right fork, turn to page 114.

In the morning, your uncle and the people in the rescue party put you on a stretcher.

"I found it," you whisper to your uncle, through bruised and swollen lips. "I found the Cave of Rushing Waters."

He pats your hand and tells you to rest.

Later, in the hospital, you ask about the source of the swift, shallow river where they found you.

"Fed by a glacier at the top of the mountain," your uncle replies, smiling. "That river was charted years ago."

"But the Cave of Rushing Waters . . ." you say. "It's *inside* that mountain."

"There is no Cave of Rushing Waters," he replies. "It's just a legend."

You lean back on the pillow. There's no use arguing, but you know better. At the top of that peak, there is a fork in the river. And more water rushes down *inside* the mountain, inside that Cathedral Room, than splashes down its rocky outer slopes.

You close your eyes. It's a secret you share with the Maoris. The Cave of Rushing Waters exists.

The End

You must defend yourself! You have one advantage: you're on dry ground. The Maori hunters are bogged down in the marsh.

You grab a fist-sized rock and take aim at the closest clump.

"Aiiiiieee!" yells the clump. An arm reaches out of the water and massages the tuft of flax.

You throw again and again, pelting the floating clumps with whatever you can grab from the shore. The waterfowl quack at the disturbance, and several parrots zoom in over the water to join the confusion.

You turn and run back to the campsite, laughing—partly in relief and partly because those big men looked so silly.

Your uncle doesn't laugh when he sees you.

"Look at your clothes!" he yells. "Where have you been?"

No point in telling the truth.

He'd never believe you.

The End

You go into the galley and open a can of beans. You even whistle while you stir in the seasoning. That's because you're seasoning it with roach powder that you found under the sink.

Babyface watches while you dish it up, but he never suspects a thing. You hand him a steaming plateful and carry two more upstairs for the other convicts.

You watch as they wolf it down eagerly—and wait for the results.

Within thirty minutes, all three are doubled up with stomach cramps. And by then your uncle has successfully started the motor.

When you get back to Te Anau, you hand the trio over to the police and book a cabin for the night.

"I'll rustle up some grub," you announce, heading inside.

Your uncle looks over at Murdoch.

"Let's eat out," he calls after you. "I'll buy."

Because of his lack of faith in your cooking, you order the biggest steak on the menu.

The End

You decide to wait in the House of Gold and see what will happen. The Tohunga didn't seem hostile—just stern. You wander around examining the intricate carvings of figures and faces and spirals on the wall posts. You think they must represent tribal ancestors. Talk about artifacts! Wait till your uncle hears about this!

A flash of light on the gold wall startles you. You whirl around as the boy from the forest enters from a side door. He slides it shut behind him. He is alone.

"Hi," you say, holding up your hand. "Who are you?"

"Wiremu," he replies, smiling.

"Why am I a hostage here, Wiremu?" you ask.

"The star—whetu," he replies, pointing skyward. "The prophecy of the star. We knew the special one would come when the star fell to the lake. It was planned in the days of our elders."

Your mind flashes back to the falling star you saw last night. Could that be what he means?

"I'm no special one!" you say emphatically. You stride toward the side door. You know it's not locked. Light is seeping in through a crack. "I'm leaving!"

"Wait!" he says, grabbing your arm. He looks frightened. You realize that he's not supposed to be here.

If you decide to leave anyway, turn to page 86.

If you stay in the House of Gold to protect Wiremu, turn to page 89.

72

The warriors form a circle around you and Hohepa.

"Your third trial awaits," says the Ariki. "When the contest is done, he who succeeds will walk into the future. He who fails will face the door of night."

Is he saying kill or be killed?

He takes the short-handled tomahawk from Hohepa's waistband and hands it to you.

You don't believe it! They expect you to kill Hohepa—with his own weapon! If you don't, you'll be killed!

Hohepa is circling you, taunting, daring you to fight. Angrily you hook the tomahawk into your belt. At least you're going to fight fair. You took a judo class at school. Maybe you can overpower him.

The people are as silent as the flickering torches they hold.

Suddenly Hohepa leaps on you and wrestles you to the ground. You roll over and over in the dirt as you try desperately to loosen his viselike grip on your arms.

Panting, covered with dust, you finally gain control. Your legs pin his arms tightly to his body. Your hands circle his neck.

Turn to page 76.

All night long you wait, nervously pacing the floor in the House of Gold. Shards of daylight are seeping through chinks in the wall when the Ariki comes. With him are two warriors, carrying the injured hunter on a litter.

One warrior brandishes his tomahawk. The other forces you to sit at the foot of the stretcher.

The Ariki faces you and speaks. "Those who betray are from a foreign tribe. Those who protect are one with us."

The warrior takes your right foot and deftly slices into your big toe with the razor-sharp blade of the tomahawk. Blood spurts out. He holds your ankle tightly and repeats the procedure on the foot of the injured man.

The Ariki kneels and presses your toe against that of his injured brother.

"Strong, silent feet carry the brave serenely through the clattering forest of life," he says. "You walk with the blood of the Tribe."

He wraps your toe in a leaf that stops the bleeding. The injured man reaches for your hand. You return his grasp with a firm squeeze.

"Go in silence," says the Ariki. "We will guide you to the trail."

He embraces you, and you see tears sparkling in his eyes.

Turn to page 88.

You tell yourself that the woman just made a lucky guess.

"How did you know I was thinking of going downstream?" you ask.

"I am burdened with knowing," she replies.

"Burdened!" you say. "I'd love to know things ahead of time. Like if your team was going to win. I think it's great!"

"You are wrong," she says solemnly. "It is not great."

"If you have second sight, why don't you know what will happen to your father?"

"With those we love, the reflection is flawed."

"Well, I don't believe in that stuff anyway," you declare.

"You must believe!" she replies. "Those who believe, grow. Those who do not, shrivel."

"What do you see for me?" you ask. "For today?"

"There are always two visions," she replies, staring off down the riverbed. "I see you running from the whip end of a storm."

"What is the other vision?" you ask, trying not to smile, for it is a beautiful day.

"That is both," she replies. "The direction in which you run is your choice. Do not follow me. *E noho ra*—goodbye."

She walks from the mound, crosses the riverbed, and quickly disappears into the forest.

If you follow the woman, turn to page 45.

If you continue your search for the boy and his dog, turn to page 56.

There's no time to leave the cave now. The floor starts to roll. A thundering roar deafens you as the avalanche advances. Small rocks and gravel come hurtling past the opening, and you run back from the entrance. You lose your balance. The cave goes dark.

Tons of gray ice and crusted snow, mixed with limestone, block the entrance.

A pale light flickers in the passageway, and you wait for the hunters to find you. As you thought, there are two of them, and the torch that one carries is faltering, for the air is thin at this altitude and the shark oil is almost consumed.

You wonder how long the oxygen in the cave will support life.

Decades later, when the cave is found, a controversy arises about the three avalanche victims. The eighteenth-century Maoris are easily identified by their spears, but when one young anthropologist insists that the third victim was a North American adolescent from the twentieth century, she is hooted out of the professional society.

As one white-haired scholar sputters: "Preposterous! What would an American youngster be doing in the Murchison Range with members of the Lost Tribe?"

What indeed?

The End

The crowd starts to chant—a frenzied, throbbing rhythm that beats in your head like a drum. Blinded by the horror of your task, you reach for the tomahawk at your waist.

You know you must kill or be killed. You avoid looking into Hohepa's eyes as he struggles for his life. You raise the weapon over your head.

Can you pass the test that means your life or his?

With a mighty heave, you hurl the tomahawk—out into space over the heads of the warriors. Then you help Hohepa to his feet.

Silence hangs heavy as a tattooed warrior approaches you. He thrusts a torch into your hand. As if by some prearranged signal, the villagers shout and leap into the air.

You back up as the crowd closes in on you. You can't defend yourself against all these people. To your right, you see a mound of dried grass up against the wooden palisade.

The confusion is frightening. Is this a celebration—or a dance of death?

The heat from the torch in your hand is singeing the hair on your arm. What should you do? If you set fire to the mound, Hohepa's whole village could burn down. But if you don't distract this mob, they might kill you.

---

*If you set fire to the mound,
turn to page 55.*

*If you stand steady as the crowd approaches,
turn to page 108.*

78

You must escape from the House of Gold!

You creep around the building, looking for an opening or a loose plank in the wall. You have just about given up hope when you notice an uneven spot in the floor near the altar. A floorboard seems to have been removed and then replaced.

You tug until it comes out. Then you slip into the space under the house, pulling the board back into place after you. As you do, you hear footsteps overhead.

Someone has entered the meetinghouse!

Loud voices and running feet tell you the search is on.

Should you stay where you are? Or should you crawl out and run for the gates?

*If you decide to stay put,
turn to page 30.*

*If you decide to crawl out and run,
turn to page 80.*

You look neither left nor right as you sprint from the House of Gold. Your mind is racing too. Perhaps this is the third test! Maybe you are *supposed* to run! Even if you don't get away, you'll still be able to barter with the Ariki for your freedom.

You veer toward the gates of the pa.

"No!" Hohepa yells from the doorway of the House of Gold. But his warning comes too late.

In the evening shadows, you never see the hardwood *taiaha*, with its tongue-shaped spearhead, thrust with lightning speed by the chief warrior. Its collar of green kaka feathers flutters frivolously in the cool breeze as you sink to the ground.

You will never find out what the third test really was.

The End

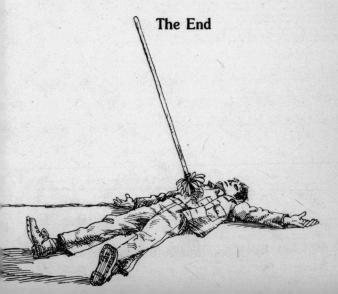

80

You dig with your hands, prying at the boards at the base of the building, and crawl through—furtively checking to see if anyone is in sight.

The coast is clear! You run for the gates—and as you do, you hear a shout. Three Maori hunters are rounding the corner of a building behind you.

Ahead is the mountain-ringed meadow. To your left, just outside the gates, is a trench—part of the fortification for the pa. Maybe you can hide in there.

Or perhaps you should run across the field. Maybe you can find the tunnel that goes back to the lake.

If you jump into the trench,
turn to page 21.

If you run across the field,
turn to page 62.

Veering left, you travel only a few hundred yards before the trench disappears into shrubbery. You push through the junglelike undergrowth. When your feet sink into the marsh, you know you're on the right track.

But you're not going to make the same mistake twice. You break a limb from a tree and prod the rushes ahead of you, searching for the snares.

Five gray ducks are floating serenely through the clumps of flax in the pond. You move quietly so you won't disturb them. Suddenly there is a flurry of wings, and four squawking ducks, unable to fly because they are moulting, move awkwardly to another section of the marsh.

You're sure *you* didn't frighten them. What did?

And wait! You turn and count again. Four ducks? What happened to the fifth?

Turn to page 101.

You whirl around and dart for the tunnel opening, the dog at your heels. You move quickly, looking back once to see if the warriors are following. You see only the golden eyes of the dog behind you.

Directly ahead, the tunnel seems brighter. Is it daylight?

No! It is fire! The Tribe has torched the exit!

You turn around and prod the dog along ahead of you. You come out of the tunnel with smarting eyes, right where you started. The warriors are waiting.

Two of them lift you by the arms and carry you into the pa, to a plot of ground with a large hole in the center. The area seems to be staked out for a new building.

Chanting priests circle the hole and move slowly toward an enormous totara tree, felled and stripped of its branches.

You've read that ancient tribes made a human sacrifice under the central pillar of a new building to ensure its safety. But that was centuries ago. Modern-day Maoris use a block of greenstone as their offering.

Turn to page 33.

You watch as the warriors return to the gates and swing them shut.

Puzzled, you crawl off, cautiously watching for a surprise attack. But none comes. It takes you three days to find your way back to Lake Te Anau. When you tell Charlie of your incredible adventure, he organizes a search to find the pa.

The search is unsuccessful. You are scolded and sent home after the University of Dunedin spends a lot of money trying to check your story.

Years later, you come across a legend that tells how a star, falling into Lake Te Anau, signified for the Maoris the arrival of a person who would lead them to victory over the white man.

That person would have to pass three tests.

You know you passed one. You spend the rest of your life wondering about the other two.

The End

Wiremu leans in through the hole, grinning. You sigh with relief. You were afraid he'd be angry because you'd been snooping.

"You take?" he asks, shoving something through the opening.

"Sure," you reply, grabbing the object.

You hold it only long enough to see what it is: a tiki—*in your image, with the eyes gouged out.*

"Wait!" you yell.

But it is too late. Already the trapdoor is being lowered into place.

You're smart. You can figure out the meaning of the double tiki. Greenstone is sacred to the Maoris. Gold is the god of the white man.

The greenstone tiki on top of the gold one represents the Maoris' superiority. And the seven eyeless tikis represent seven other adventurers who found the Lost Tribe of Fiordland—but never lived to tell the tale.

Now there are eight.

The End

"I'm not staying here!" you say to Wiremu.

You open the side door and step outside the House of Gold. No one is around. You take three steps and feel the ground give way under your feet. Down, down you fall, landing on soft soil at the bottom of a pit.

You claw at the walls, trying to scale them, but the dirt only crumbles in on top of you. You try again. More dirt falls. Soon you are buried to your knees.

The voice of the Tohunga drifts down to you as you try to free your legs.

"He who denies the prophecy digs his own grave. Your deliverance will be your doom."

He leaves. You push his strange words from your mind. You concentrate on staying very still to prevent more earth from falling in. Your uncle will look for you! You can survive without food until he finds you. You know that. But you need water. If only it would rain.

The days are hot. No one comes near the pit. You lose track of time. All you can think of is water.

Then, late on the third night, you hear thunder. A downpour! Rain drenches you. You cup your hands and drink eagerly.

But the water that is saving you from sure death is also caving in the sides of the pit. Soon you are buried to your waist. Now you know what the Tohunga meant.

Your deliverance will be your doom.

The End

When you finally get back to camp, you make up a story about being lost. Your uncle Charlie says that it's a common occurrence in Fiordland.

But there was nothing common about your experience in that beautiful wild country. Whenever you look at the scar on your toe, you remind yourself with pride that you are the only pakeha on earth who shares the blood—and the secret—of the Lost Tribe of Fiordland.

The End

"Wait!" Wiremu repeats urgently. "Shadows come."

"All right," you reply.

Wiremu has a point. You should wait for nightfall. You'll never get out of the pa unnoticed in daylight.

"Food?" you say to him, rubbing your stomach.

"Ah," he replies, nodding.

He moves to the door and leaves the meetinghouse quietly, sliding the door shut behind him. You decide to do some more exploring while you wait.

As you investigate the area by the altar, you notice a large metal ring attached to the floor. Curious, you tug at it. A section of the floor lifts up like a trapdoor, and you see roughly hewn steps leading down into the ground.

It could be a secret passage leading out of the pa—or maybe it's a storage room for more gold!

On the other hand, it could be a trap.

If you decide to go down the steps,
turn to page 34.

If you decide to wait for Wiremu,
turn to page 38.

This is no time to run. There are too many armed warriors in the circle. And it's too far back to the tunnel.

Suddenly all activity stops. Even the dog drops, whimpering, to a crouching position.

Approaching you is the Tohunga—the wise man of the tribe—carrying a carved stick that is taller than he is. Your uncle showed you one of these. It is a *rakau whaka-papa*, the tribal tree or genealogical history of the tribe.

"Go!" says the Tohunga to the warriors.

They move quietly toward the pa as he stares at you.

His face is heavily tattooed, and two feathers jut up from the back of his white hair. He is tall and broad. His powerful arms look as if they have downed many foes. Sharks' teeth hang from his pierced ears; a cape of flax fibers is attached over his left shoulder.

"Come!" he says.

You have no intention of disobeying. The dog follows as the Tohunga leads you into the pa.

Turn to page 39.

Impossible or not, you decide to take the injured man with you back through the tunnel to the pa. You lash together a makeshift litter using flax from his skirt and vines from the mountainside.

Slowly you start the long trek back through the passageway, dragging the litter behind you. Your hands grow raw from the tough vines. Your shoulders ache from the strain of pulling the huge man.

Finally you see a glimmer of light ahead. You are approaching the entrance!

Will the Tribe kill you before you can tell them you have brought back one of their injured brothers?

You stop just short of the end of the tunnel to think. You need something to show them why you're back. Your eyes light on the red kaka feathers sticking out from the hunter's hair. You remove them and place them in your own tousled locks.

Then you step to the tunnel opening, cautiously watching for Maori scouts. Your alertness pays off. One jumps from the bushes, wielding his greenstone *mere*, and you step quickly aside. He crashes to the dirt at the tunnel entrance.

When he sees the red feathers, he whistles once. Another scout joins him.

You point to the tunnel opening. They enter quickly to help their injured friend.

Turn to page 10.

The cavern is now as black as a moonless night. The warrior who was holding your ankles has taken the last flickering torch from the wall and left the cave. You think you are alone, but you're afraid to move. You lie very still for a while and then cautiously sit up and reach for your shoes and socks.

If you can just find that passageway! You feel your way to the ledge where the Tohunga was seated with the little boy, and you spy an opening in the rock.

Within minutes, you are racing through the forest toward Lake Te Anau.

Not until morning do you see the Maoris' handiwork.

Tattooed on the sole of each foot is a bright blue arrow—pointing backward.

You vow never to run from opportunity again.

The End

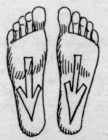

You place your rolled-up flannel shirt under the head of the injured hunter. Then you build a channel of rocks and packed snow around his mangled leg to keep it steady.

"I'll be back soon," you say. "I'm going back to the pa."

His eyes flicker open and a worried expression crosses his face. *"Tao,"* he whispers, gesturing toward the cave.

Of course! He knows they'll kill you if you return alone. But if you're carrying his spear, the Tribe may give you a chance to explain.

You dig through the debris at the cave's entrance until you find the weapon. The shaft is broken, but the top section with the bone barb is intact. You pull it from the rubble and move through the tunnel toward the pa.

Two scouts are posted at the meadow entrance. One leaps toward you.

"The hunter is injured," you say quickly, holding up the spear.

The broken weapon stops him, and the scouts hurry back to the injured man with you.

They lash together a crude stretcher from vines. With you leading, they carry him through the tunnel and across the meadow.

Turn to page 27.

Escape should be easy, you think. You've already escaped from the House of Gold once. They must have poor memories!

You yank up the floorboard and crawl through. But the hole you dug in the foundation has been filled in with heavy rocks. You move to another spot to dig. More rocks!

Frantic, you try other places. The whole inside of the building has been braced with chunks of limestone. You rush back to the loose floorboard. You must get back inside the house!

But the board will not budge. You bang and hammer with your fists. You shout and yell. The floor has been sealed shut.

You sit back on your heels in the dirt under the house and listen to the noises of the night.

In the morning, the Ariki and his warriors come and remove the floorboard, releasing you from your prison under the house. Silently they lead you across the meadow and through the tunnel. Then they disappear into the forest without a word.

You spend many days looking, without success, for your campsite. Growing weaker, you struggle through the rough terrain. You are hopelessly lost.

The last things you see are the harrier hawks—the *kahu* of the Maoris—circling overhead, waiting for dinner.

The End

"What are the other two tests?" you ask Hohepa nervously.

"The first test you know, for you have passed it," he replies.

"Escaping from here? Was that the first one?"

"Partly."

"The third?" you say.

You detect a flash of fear in Hohepa's eyes.

"I am forbidden to speak of it," he says softly. He stands up. "It is time for the evening meal. I will bring food."

He returns with a wooden bowl full of stew and some warm bread wrapped in leaves.

You stare at the food, wondering if it is poisoned. But your fears disappear when you realize that Hohepa will share it with you.

He unties your hands and you eat together like longtime friends. When you finish eating, you sit together in companionable silence. You like this quiet Maori boy, and you wish your worlds were not so far apart. Hohepa sighs, as though reading your mind.

"It is time," he says finally, getting up. He leans over and slices through the vines binding your feet. His hand lingers on yours as he pulls you up. Then, with one quick squeeze, he releases his hold. "Come."

You know it is time for the third test. This may be your last chance. Should you follow him? Or should you run when he opens the door?

If you run, turn to page 79.

If you follow Hohepa, turn to page 23.

You rush back to the ledge. You're determined to tell everyone about your find. Let your uncle settle for cracked moa eggs and hunting knives! You have found the legendary Glowing Caves! Perhaps the government will name them after you! Your name and your picture will be in the papers! You'll be a celebrity!

Filled with visions of grandeur, you become careless. In your rush for fame, your foot slips from the ledge. You plunge hundreds of feet down to instant death.

Years later, the Glowing Caves are discovered by someone else, and scientists explain the mysterious lights.

It's not phosphorus in the rock, as you thought, but *worms*—millions of tiny glowworms—lighting the spectacular grotto in the Caves of Te Ana-au.

Your mysterious disappearance, however, is never explained.

The End

The villagers have formed a circle around the water trough in front of the gates of the pa. You strain to look over the heads of the crowd to see what is causing the excitement. A young woman is holding the limp body of a small boy, who is dripping with water. He must have fallen into the trough!

You earned your Red Cross certificate in artificial respiration last summer. Maybe you should try to help.

On the other hand, nobody has even noticed you, and the gates to freedom are only a few feet away.

If you decide to help, turn to page 103.

If you decide to run for the gates, turn to page 66.

You count the ducks again. Four. As you wonder what happened to the fifth duck, you see a clump of flax floating toward you. Two clumps. Three! But there is no wind!

You start to run—which is hard to do when you're ankle deep in sludge. You look back. The three clumps are gaining on you.

You reach solid ground just as one of the clumps rises out of the water. Underneath the flax is a Maori hunter. Attached to his waist is the fifth duck. The other two clumps are rising. You don't need to look to know what's under them.

Can you run fast enough to escape—or should you defend yourself?

If you decide to run, turn to page 17.

*If you decide to defend yourself,
turn to page 68.*

The damp air penetrates your clothing as you move along the left fork, and the darkness is spooky. Something brushes up against your head.

A bat, you think, and proceed even more carefully. Now and again a glimpse of daylight seeps through a crack, but there is no opening large enough for you to get even an arm through, let alone your body.

It occurs to you that you're inside a mountain. The thought is chilling. What if there is an earthquake? You push the idea aside.

The path narrows, and your foot suddenly slips off into emptiness. You are moving on a narrow ledge. Below you, on the right, is a deep chasm.

Is there water down there?

You pick up a stone and drop it into black space.

Moments later, you hear a soft splash. It's a long way down. But it might be a route to the outside! The water has to come from somewhere!

If you decide to climb down to the water, turn to page 19.

If you decide to keep following the ledge, turn to page 24.

You push your way through the crowd and quickly take the boy from his mother. You strike him sharply on the back to be sure his air passage is clear.

The crowd becomes ominously silent. Your heart pounds.

You lay him out on the ground and start blowing air into his mouth. You watch his chest rise and then fall; then you remove your mouth so the air can be exhaled.

Over and over again you repeat your movements.

The crowd is murmuring, but the only noise you hear is the choking sound of the child as he starts to breathe on his own.

You sit down quickly, knees weak, watching with a silly grin as his mother snatches him up and covers him with kisses. But your rest is short-lived. Coming toward you are two of the biggest warriors of the Tribe.

Turn to page 112.

You have to think fast. You can't physically overpower three men. Use your wits! The woman upstream was superstitious. Maybe these hunters are too!

You dig into your pockets. Sunglasses, a flashlight, bubble gum, some pebbles. You make a plan.

Your sunglasses have reflective glass. No one can see your eyes through the lenses. You slip them on and turn on your flashlight. Then, rattling the pebbles in your hand, you walk into the clearing.

The man with the leather thong whips around at the noise. As he turns, you shine your flashlight into his face and blow a beautiful pink bubble that covers your face from your chin to the glasses. You hope you look like something from Mars.

With a wild cry, he bolts for the forest, followed by the others. You hurry over and untie the boy. But before you can ask him any questions, he darts into the undergrowth like a frightened animal.

You don't dare follow him now. The hunters may not stay gone for long. But you plan to do some searching tomorrow.

You return to the campsite. Your uncle Charlie and Murdoch are just docking the boat.

"I hope you won't be bored over here," your uncle says.

"Oh, I'll find things to keep me busy," you answer, blowing a big pink bubble.

The End

The ranger's storehouse door is locked, so you hoist yourself up to look in a window. A gruff voice behind you makes you lose your grip.

"We've got you covered, Babyface!"

You drop to the ground. Two policemen and a ranger are aiming their guns at you.

"I'm not Babyface," you say, turning so they can see your face. "He's over there. He has speargrass cuts and sand fly bites."

You and the officers escort him to the launch, where they arrest the other two convicts as well.

When you, Uncle Charlie, and Murdoch get safely back to Te Anau, you rent a cabin for the night. You ask your uncle to get the sleeping bags from the launch. A sheepish look crosses his face. You know what that look means.

"Forget it," you say.

"Right," says your forgetful uncle. "I'll get them tomorrow when we go back."

Murdoch looks over at you and manages a weak grin.

"If he can remember," he mutters.

The End

You dart back into the tunnel. If you can reach the other fork, you might be able to escape the warriors. You think the other passage probably leads to the forest.

You start to run. The sound of your heavy breathing bounces off the walls. You reach the fork and hurry along the narrow path. Ahead you can see light! The setting sun shines down on the rich green of the forest.

Jubilant, you race for the opening. You are so intent on freedom that you don't even see the five-foot chasm that splits the trail.

Down, down, down you go, spinning like a top—into the glacier waters of the bottomless pool inside the mountain.

Your mysterious disappearance is never explained. The tribal council adjourns, and life in the pa continues as usual.

The Lost Tribe of Fiordland is never discovered.

The End

You stand firm, facing the swarm of noisy villagers. Suddenly the mob divides down the middle. The Ariki approaches you slowly. He takes the torch from your hand and holds it aloft. You stiffen your back, waiting for him to signal your execution.

"You have passed the three tests," he says gravely.

You stare at him, unbelieving.

"First," he continues, "the test of cunning bonded to honesty—for you escaped from the House of Gold, yet stole not our treasures."

The circle of villagers closes in.

"Second, the test of bravery coupled with compassion—for you saved the child of your enemy."

The flickering torches are so close now that you can feel their warmth and smell the shark oil that keeps them flaming.

"Third," he continues, "the test of fairness mated to mercy—for you took not the life of your unarmed friend. You are indeed the promised one. *Whetu!*"

Hohepa grips you in a crushing hug, which you return joyfully.

"Whetu, whetu," the crowd chants, and the frenzied dancing begins again.

Go on to the next page.

A great feast is prepared. The celebrations last far into the night. But your problems are not solved. At dawn, you approach the Ariki.

"What is your wish?" the stately man asks.

"To return to my people," you say. "I appreciate all this, but I am not Whetu. I cannot help you to regain your lost lands."

His eyes narrow, and you think for a moment that you have destroyed your last chance to ever leave the Tribe.

"The cloak is woven before the border is added," he says. "You are one with us. I will not fight the gods. Go. Work for us where you will."

The next morning, Hohepa leads you through the tunnel to the meadow. Before you part, he gives you his tomahawk. You give him your class ring.

You tell your uncle nothing of your strange adventure, but merely say that you got lost—and found the tomahawk in the wilds.

Years later, you become a citizen of New Zealand and are elected to Parliament. You are instrumental in passing a bill that gives great tracts of land back to the Maoris.

The Ariki's prophecy is fulfilled.

The End

110

You stand—and two warriors move swiftly to flank you. They guide you along the length of the deep cavern—past the silent Maori fighters, past a rock slab table where two ornately tattooed warriors stand—until you reach the base of the Tohunga's platform. The flickering torches cast eerie shadows at your feet.

The Tohunga rises. He slams the tribal stick on the ground.

"He who runs from opportunity travels backward!"

His deep voice echoes in the rock room. The warriors pick you up and carry you to the slab. Are they going to kill you?

You are placed face down, and your shoes and socks are removed. In the flickering light, you see one of the warriors pick up a miniature adze—a tiny ax—made of bone. Another carries a bowl of something.

Someone grabs your ankles. You stifle an involuntary giggle. The Maoris are tickling your feet!

You peek up. The men who were encircling the room are filing out through an opening behind the Tohunga's platform. Each man takes the torch he is carrying, plus one from the wall. The cave is growing dim.

The firm hold on your ankles is released.

Turn to page 93.

112

The warriors swoop down on you, lifting you up over their heads in a gesture of triumph.

The Tohunga puts a wreath of small white flowers on your head, like a crown. Then the warriors, with the villagers following, carry you to the square, where you are placed in a handsome carved chair on stilts.

Food is quickly prepared for a feast. Women poi dancers, cheeks streaked with black and red paint, sway gracefully to music played on a short stick that is held between the teeth and twanged with the hand.

It's getting dark. You've got to get out of here. Your uncle will be worried. Wiremu is nowhere in sight.

A tall cut sapling is leaning against the side of your elevated chair. Should you try to escape now, at the height of the festivities—or wait till you find Wiremu? You're pretty sure he'll help you.

If you decide to use the sapling to escape now, turn to page 31.

If you wait to find Wiremu, turn to page 46.

114

The silence is eerie as you move along the right fork inside the tunnel. The place is well insulated. The loose rock and reddish earth you saw farther back have turned into massive sheets of stone, visible only when occasional shafts of light arrow in through openings high above your head.

The farther you go, the darker it becomes. You finally realize that you are inside the mountain!

Groping your way, you follow the path around a corner. Through a low opening ahead, you can see light! Is it daylight?

You crawl through and are temporarily blinded by the glare. Hundreds of flaming torches dot the walls of a huge cavern. Dozens more are held aloft by wildly tattooed Maori warriors who line the walls.

The tribal council has assembled, and they are expecting you.

Turn to page 35.

You make your decision quickly. You must run!

The Ariki puts out his arms. You hand him the little girl. This is even better than you had hoped. He can't chase you carrying a child!

You turn and dash to the nearest section of the wall, hoping to scale it. You don't get far. The Ariki's piercing whistle cuts through the village silence like a saber. Immediately you are surrounded by chanting Maori warriors.

The Ariki holds up his hand and the chanting stops.

"This is not the promised star," he says. "This one—though brave through billowing clouds—runs like a rat for the fence. . . . Out!"

What does he mean by star?

The Ariki waves his hand toward the gates. Two of the largest warriors pick you up and carry you through, dumping you unceremoniously on the ground outside.

Are they going to kill you?

Turn to page 84.

You scramble up the slope. You've made it, all right. You're back at the gates—right where you started. And the Tribe has a reception committee waiting.

You are hustled off to the center of the square. Your hair is shaved off; your neck and arms are stained with yellow ocher.

Then the tribe presents you with a gift. A sturdy hardwood shovel. Remember all those trenches you wondered about?

You were right. They hadn't heard of bulldozers.

Now you know how the trenches were excavated.

After ten years with the tribe, you work your way out of slave status and become a villager. Life is not too bad. You fish and hunt, and you don't miss civilization very much.

But every once in a while, you venture back to the forest and bury a shark's tooth or a bone carving tool in the soil under the ferns.

You like to think of your uncle out there finding them.

The End

ABOUT THE AUTHOR

LOUISE MUNRO FOLEY is the author of nine books for young readers and has won several national awards for writing and editing. In addition to writing, she has hosted shows on radio and television in the United States and Canada. She has also written a newspaper column, and her articles have appeared in the *Christian Science Monitor, The Horn Book,* and *Writer's Digest.* A native of Toronto, Ontario, Canada, Ms. Foley now lives in Sacramento, California. She and her husband have two sons.

ABOUT THE ILLUSTRATOR

PAUL GRANGER is a prize-winning illustrator and painter.